D1343446

A mouse-eye view of the founding of the Royal Observatory

By Frances Willmoth

Illustrated by Audrey Sansick and the author

2016

Dedicated

to the staff of the National Maritime Museum (Royal Museums Greenwich),
especially the custodians of Flamsteed House,
and to the memory of John Sansick, playwright, author of the plays 'Flamsteed' and 'Hooke'

Acknowledgements

We are very grateful to the National Maritime Museum
and to the Master and Fellows of Magdalene College, Cambridge,
for permission to use and adapt some of Francis Place's
engravings of the Royal Observatory held in their collections.

The illustrator is very grateful to Kiran Sharma and Tracy Tunstall,
librarians at Hanwell Library, for their kind assistance.

The author would like to thank her niece, Emily Willmoth, for comments on a first draft of this book.

Published by Frances Willmoth

Designed and set by Nikki Williams, Jesus College, Cambridge

Printed and bound in Great Britain by Swan Print Ltd, Bedford

ISBN 978-1-5262-0605-3

CONTENTS

CHAPTER 1

In which the mice of Greenwich Hill meet some humans with plans to change everything

"Watch out! Feet on the hill! Humans! Hide fast! Keep quiet!" These squeaks of alarm from a lookout mouse alerted the others who were browsing around on the upper slopes of Greenwich Hill looking for snacks, and soon they could all hear the sound of approaching footsteps and a murmur of voices.

It was a chilly morning in early spring, in the year 1675. The colony of mice who lived in the ancient, ruined building called the Castle, at the top of the hill, usually explored further down, where there was more chance that someone might have walked by dropping crumbs of bread or biscuit. But on this particular day the weather was so grey, damp and mizzly that none of them felt like venturing far from their nests. Some had stayed very close to home, and could easily hide in the long grass and weeds around the Castle, so they had the chance to take a close look at the visitors and to listen to their conversation.

First came a small, spry, lively-looking man, striding up the hill with an energetic and commanding air and glancing keenly about him. Last came a taller, older, stouter man, plodding up the path with the help of a cane. Between the two was a youngish one, maybe in his late twenties, who walked briskly but in fits and starts. He often turned round and paused as if to look at the view, to give the older man time to catch up.

That day there wasn't much of a view to enjoy at all. The Queen's House, close by at the foot of the hill, looked solid enough, but the King's unfinished new palace building beyond it was half hidden in mist. The great river Thames stretched out dimly beyond them, with a few shapes of ships passing slowly up and down it, but the mistiness of the air made the towers and spires of London, away to the West, completely invisible.

When the three visitors had reached the top of the hill and paused to catch their breath, the small man led them off on a tour around the outside of the ruins. They had to step over a few brambles (and a few mice) along the way. They all seemed to be looking very closely at what was left of the building, although it was not much more than an overgrown pile of rubble; the stout man prodded it with his cane from time to time, with a doubtful expression on his face. The youngish one walked a little way behind the other two, looking thoughtful and a little anxious. When they had completed the circuit he caught the others up again and they all turned and faced the mound of rubble together.

"This is a fine and honest hill, Sir Christopher," said the stout man, "and I see why you chose it. But it's a long way from the City and the Court, and there's not much left of this building that we can use. Rebuilding will be expensive."

"But Joney," came the reply, "the Ordnance Office has promised some cash – five hundred pounds is not to be sneezed at. And now the Dutch war is over the Office has little to do, so it should be able to find some materials too. We might be able to reuse some of the old bricks here and I believe there are some lying around spare at Tilbury. I'm sure we can pick up lead for the roofs somewhere – perhaps from those storehouses that are being demolished at the Tower? And rebuilding won't be such a bad thing. We can make two of the walls run north-to-south, in alignment with the meridian. Or at least we can put in *one* meridian wall somewhere convenient for your instruments."

The young man here looked a little worried, and said "Better the main walls, if it can be managed, Sir Christopher, surely." Sir Christopher did not respond, but the stout man nodded reassuringly.

"As for the distance," Sir Christopher continued, "being well away from London will bring the astronomer great benefits. It's bad enough having to wait for the English weather to allow you a clear sky without having to wait for a strong wind too, to blow the smoke away. I believe you have had experience of that, at Derby, Flamsteed."

The young man agreed, with a sigh, then added: "We also have a river in Derby, and it creates damp air as the Thames does. And, Sir Jonas, you know that, when we've been observing in the Tower, we've often had trouble with the damp rising from the river misting our telescope lenses. Are you sure the same problem won't occur here? It would have been far drier in Hyde Park." "Perhaps so," said Sir Jonas, "but there an East wind would have blown the city smoke over everything often enough. And I believe this hill is high enough to lift you well above most of the river mists."

"Yes indeed," said Sir Christopher. "And the observatory – your *royal* observatory, Sir Jonas – will become very well known if it's placed here. It will be a splendid landmark, as everyone will see it as they travel down river or take ship at Greenwich to sail the oceans. It will be big enough to look dignified and for the astronomer to live in. Of course it can't be as large and grand as the Paris Observatory – we don't have Louis XIV as our master."

"Praise God for that!", said Sir Jonas, and he and Sir Christopher laughed; even Flamsteed smiled briefly. Then they turned and set off back down the hill.

CHAPTER 2

In which the mice worry about their future
and are persuaded to learn from history

As soon as the visitors had gone out of earshot, the mice hurried to gather in a sheltered spot at the back of the ruin. Some were in a state of great consternation; some were a little flustered; some were just puzzled. They were soon all agreed that it really did sound as though their ruined building was going to be cleared away and replaced with something new. There was much worried shaking of heads and muttering over how they were going to live if such a dreadful thing happened to their nesting-places. Perhaps they'd all have to move back down the hill into Greenwich? There were too many other mice down there already, and far too many cats. The comment that such an upheaval had never been known before was heard more than once.

After a while the history mouse of that time, Clarinda, cut in to the conversation. "Nonsense," she said firmly, "it *has* happened before. Humans can never be content with what they have, and they like to keep busy by knocking things down and rebuilding them. Just think about what's happened to the view from the top of our hill! Mice (field mice, at least) were here before any humans, and everything was green then, but you know there's been a royal mansion house down by the river for at least a thousand years.

"At first it was like a great barn – not bad for mice as there was a store for grain and flour and a lot of bread baked. But then people came and cut some big trees down, and floated some more down the river, and rebuilt it as a proper house with rooms and floorboards. The mice were shocked and upset at first, but soon found their new quarters a great improvement. And maybe one of the master

builders brought some spare wood up the hill to make a hut, and that was when a few of us house mice first left the riverside.

"Later the famous Duke Humphrey of Gloucester took charge." (There was a murmur of puzzlement – "who?" – "famous?" – "never heard of him" – and some stopped listening.) "Duke Humphrey turned the half-timbered house into a stone palace, and started building a stone tower here on the hill. His huntsman used it sometimes, and people from the palace came by when they were hunting and picnicking in the park.

"From that time to the present, a flourishing mouse settlement has been firmly established here." (Some of the audience here clapped and cheered, so the mice who'd stopped listening started paying attention again.) "The tower made a good perch for owls, which has sometimes made life hazardous, but the advantages of having shelter and occasional supplies of human food far outweighed this minor problem.

"After Duke Humphrey died, the kings took Greenwich Palace for themselves and changed it around some more. Henry VII finished off our tower and Henry VIII added to it to make it more comfortable for his huge hunting parties and his lady friends. The building work must have been a horrible nuisance for a while – very noisy in the daytime, when mice prefer to get some sleep. But it turned out to be a good thing in the end.

"The mice not only ate the crumbs from the workmen's bread and cheese, but had a really good time when the building started to be lived in properly. Henry VIII's ladies didn't have much to do but plan meals and parties and picnics, and test the menus when they were feeling bored, so there was always wonderful food to be had.

"The owls were disturbed by there being so many people about, and moved back over to Blackheath for some peace. That was a real golden age!

"And then it changed again, when James I had the house rebuilt and gave it to the Ranger of Greenwich Park to live in. The mice of those times had to put up with a lot of dust and dirt and muddle, but eventually there were some fine rooms with loose enough skirting-boards for mice to slip around and a table big enough for a real banquet.

"It was only very recently, with the dreadful Civil War and Oliver Cromwell, that the people went away and the house was left to fall down. For a short while it was used for making biscuits for soldiers' rations, so we didn't go hungry but the food was very dull. It was cheap flour, you see, and tended to get damp before they cooked it; and the biscuits were baked very hard. And then even that stopped and for a long while now we have had to go out into the park to find food."

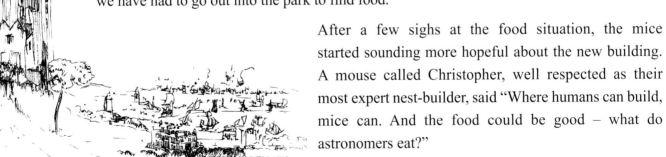

After a few sighs at the food situation, the mice started sounding more hopeful about the new building. A mouse called Christopher, well respected as their most expert nest-builder, said "Where humans can build, mice can. And the food could be good – what do astronomers eat?"

CHAPTER 3

In which the mice learn more about the designs for a new observatory

After that, nothing happened for so long that most of the mice forgot about the visitors; any who remembered assumed the humans had changed their minds. The hill's trees put out their leaves and the sun came out from time to time. People were occasionally seen wandering around in the park (with or without official permission), and eventually the midsummer picnicking season arrived. This was definitely the favourite time for the mice, as the usual wild boys running about and strollers from Greenwich were joined by courtiers and their friends coming down-river from London. These festive parties brought lavish food supplies with them and happily had a careless approach to eating.

One early morning, on a breezy day a few days after midsummer, the mice were pottering about looking for scraps of food at the top of the giant green steps just to one side of the hill. The remains of a particularly good picnic were to be found there. (The menu had included pork pies and venison pasties, hard-boiled eggs, cucumber salad, strawberries, shortbread, honeycakes and gingerbread.) From that ideal vantage-point, one of the mice suddenly spotted a group of men behaving rather oddly. Two of them were walking about briskly at the foot of the hill and pausing sometimes to look at it; two more, dressed like workmen, were standing about watching. In the pauses one of the brisk two seemed to be writing notes. Then they started climbing the hill in a zigzag fashion, again stopping from time to time to look up towards the top, and beckoning the workmen to follow.

As they came closer, the mice realised that the one without the notebook was the young man who had visited before, the one called Flamsteed. He looked more cheerful than he had the last time.

The two men paused for a few moments at the top of the giant grass steps, looking across at the hilltop and the Castle ruin. "It's a fine site for the building, Mr Hooke," said Flamsteed, "and I hope it will be spacious enough for all our needs. The King expects his new astronomical observator to be well accommodated."

"Indeed," said his companion, sounding a little irritated, "Sir Christopher himself, when he handed his design to me and gave me the task of directing the building, had those same priorities – he said it will be 'for the observer's habitation and a little for pomp'. And we shall be ready to start on the work in just a few days, as fast as His Majesty or anyone else could wish."

Then they set off southwards towards the Blackheath gate of the park. Part-way there they turned to look back at the hilltop and Hooke brought out his notebook once more.

When they came back again to the ruin, they walked round it to the front of the site, overlooking the river. As it was a clear, bright day this time, the views of London and of the shining Thames stretching away eastward towards the sea were quite spectacular. The men paused to look for just a moment, then from the heavy leather satchel that one of the workmen carried they extracted a long coiled-up metal chain. They unwound it, taking one end each, then spread it out carefully in a straight line alongside the rubble. Hooke noted something down and then they moved the chain to measure another, longer line a few feet in front of the first one.

"I had hopes," said Flamsteed, "that we should not have to use exactly the same frontage, but could cut across it and have side walls in the meridian." "No hope of that," came the reply. "Not for the sum of money the Ordnance Office is willing to pay. And in any case it would spoil the appearance if the building didn't lie parallel to the Queen's House and the river. We shall build a separate meridian wall in a house of its own in the Observatory's garden, which will be much more practical for the new mural quadrant than trying to fit it into the main building. And the sextant can be housed there too." Flamsteed sighed but nodded, and said "so long as it's a proper instrument-house, not just a shed."

A few mice nodded too, thinking this all sounded quite promising in terms of mouse-friendly accommodation. And they greatly approved of the idea of reusing the old foundations, as perhaps it would allow some of their old nests to be preserved.

"And then," said Hooke, "the main building will suit all your other purposes. Sir Christopher had a fancy for octagonal towers like the Paris Observatory's, but he settled in the end for just the one central room being octagonal. There isn't a wide enough space here to have a frontage with large towers, in any case. It will have to be fairly plain, but the octagonal room behind it will have long windows facing in several directions. Those can take telescopes, so you won't always have to work outside. And it will be a high-ceilinged room, so it can house our new clocks with long pendulums, built in behind the wainscot."

"The windows may be some use," said Flamsteed, sounding doubtful, "and the clocks will truly be extraordinarily fine, if Mr Tompion does his work well. It may be awkward to carry the time from them to

another clock standing alongside the instruments in the garden, but it can be done. Sir Jonas is very generous, so I'm sure he can spare a few pounds for an extra clock."

The mice became a little agitated at this point, because Hooke was talking about putting clocks behind the wainscot. Wainscot is a word mice always like to hear, as it means there's a lot of space for them to creep about in unseen, but how on earth could anyone put clocks behind it? Pendulum clocks hadn't been seen on Greenwich Hill before - they had only been invented a few years before – but the mice who'd set foot in the town had seen ordinary clocks and claimed there were one or two like large cupboards that rattled a lot and chimed a bell for the hours. Perhaps that was the kind of thing Hooke was planning? And in that case might it make the whole building too noisy to live in?

When they started listening again, Hooke had moved on to other subjects. "Sir Jonas has ordered some lenses for long telescopes from Paris, I believe," he said, "and those you can set up on the roof. Hevelius shows how to do that in the pictures of his observatory in Danzig."

"It will be a flat roof, then?" said Flamsteed. "Yes," said Hooke, "but, to improve the appearance, there will be turrets on either side. An echo of the Tower of London, to please Sir Jonas and the Ordnance Office, and perhaps to remind you of your quarters in the White Tower."

"Less than ideal quarters, as you saw when you visited me," said Flamsteed. "I shan't be sorry to leave them. I'm told I can come down and work at the Queen's House instead, when the building starts here. Then I can help keep an eye on the builders, too." Hooke nodded but said no more. He and Flamsteed dragged the chain around the corner and measured a long line down the side of the plot, before coiling it up again, returning it to the satchel and setting off back down the hill to Greenwich.

CHAPTER 4

In which a fence is set up around the hilltop site and the mice begin to worry again

It was only about a week later that Hooke quietly appeared again, this time with a tall, stately, official-looking man, who wore a heavy wig despite the warm weather and carried a roll of paper and a large notebook.

At the top of the hill they stopped and looked at the view towards the river with its crowd of ships, then back at the park. The tall man unrolled the paper, which appeared to be some sort of plan. The few mice watching them from the shade of the ruins could only catch a few words as the tall man and Hooke talked together earnestly. He appeared to say something severe and Hooke said "Don't worry, Sir Edward, I'm very well aware." As Hooke talked on, gesturing once or twice towards the ruins, Sir Edward scribbled in his notebook.

SIR EDWARD SHERBURNE

A couple of the mice, knowing that the quietest conversations are often the most important, decided to creep closer. They saw Sir Edward tap his pencil down a row of figures in the notebook, as though adding them up, and then he said "it looks as though it's within the five hundred pounds now, but it must stay there. Don't come to me in six months time with alterations and additions to make it six hundred."

"No, indeed," said Hooke in soothing tones, "the design is already agreed and there can be no reason to change anything." "Then we can start building straight away," said Sir Edward, "and perhaps get the roof on by Christmas."

"That will depend on your workmen, of course," said Hooke. "If they work hard and don't get called away on other projects, and if the weather is kind to us, we should have a roof before Easter."

The mice who'd heard all this immediately rushed back and spread alarm amongst the rest: the new building really was going to happen, and starting very soon. Some of them began planning to run away, back down the hill – to the town of Greenwich, or perhaps to the Queen's House or half-built King's House as quieter options. And then an elderly mouse wisely pointed out that in human terms "starting straight away" didn't always mean tomorrow, or even this week. So the jitters died down again.

Another week or so passed peacefully enough, with small outbreaks of worry disturbing the mice not more than once or twice a day. Then, one sunny morning, heavy footsteps and some rattling noises were heard close by. A group of workmen were walking up the hill, along with Sir Edward, Sir Jonas, Hooke and Flamsteed.

The workmen trudged slowly, carrying spades, a sledge-hammer and a sack of small tools; several shouldered bundles of wooden stakes, one had a long pole marked with black and white stripes, and two carried a wooden box carefully between them. There was also a boy with a large wicker basket, and another rolling a small keg up the hill.

When they all reached the top, the keg was perched on a pile of rubble. Most of the workmen dumped their burdens and sat down on the grass, but the ones with the wooden box set it down gently and opened it.

Any mice in the neighbourhood immediately started paying close attention. Having seen the keg and worked out that it probably contained beer, they were hopeful that the box might produce a picnic. The humans certainly seemed to be very interested in it: Hooke came over to supervise, with Sir Jonas, Sir Edward and Flamsteed watching closely.

First the workmen took out a wooden tripod and set it up on its legs. Then some shiny brass pieces were unpacked and Hooke fitted them together carefully on top of the tripod. There was a circular piece as a base, and a kind of semicircle above it, hanging from a stand. He and Sir Jonas together carefully lifted up the tripod and carried it over to stand near to one corner of the ruins, then Hooke peered across the top of the instrument in different directions, mostly towards the river. He beckoned to Flamsteed to bring over the rolled-up plan, unrolled it and looked at it, then looked at the instrument again. Then he moved the tripod a foot or two one way and peered again, and a foot or two another way and peered again, and then he seemed happy with it.

He called to a workman and had him hammer in a short wooden stake in between the legs of the tripod, to mark the spot. Then he made another workman hold the stripy pole some distance away, past the front of the ruins, waving to him to move it to and fro until it was on exactly the right line. Another workman unrolled a surveying chain from the marker towards the pole and measured a distance, and another short stake was driven

into the ground at that spot. And then Hooke and Sir Jonas carried the tripod and the instrument over and put it down exactly above the stake.

After that all that happened was more of the same: Hooke and Sir Jonas and the instrument went round all the corners of the plot of ground until they got back to where they started. By then the mice had almost lost interest, but they paid attention again when the workmen started replacing the short stakes with fenceposts and putting up fences on every side of the plot. These changed the look of the place in rather a shocking way, but fortunately turned out to be very rough fences with plenty of spaces big enough for mice to squeeze through.

There was a gate included too, so when the fencing was done the workmen could use it to retrieve their keg of beer. They fished some tankards out of a sack and a generous supply of pies and pasties out of the wicker basket, and sat down to eat and drink. There were plenty of pastry-crumbs left for the mice to enjoy once everyone had left.

CHAPTER 5

In which the mice move down the hill and take refuge in the Queen's House

The mood amongst the mice was now very gloomy. They were going to have to find somewhere else to live very quickly, as the humans really were going to start clearing and rebuilding. No-one could guess how long it might be before everything was well enough finished for a move back. "If it's like the King's House," one mouse said, "it might stop part-way through and never get finished at all. And then what shall we do?" "But that was because the King ran out of money," said an adventurous mouse who'd been down to the town and heard the gossip. "It sounds as though that won't happen here, so long as Mr Hooke sticks to the plan and doesn't try to spend too much." "If the worst comes to the worst," said a joker, "Sir Edward can just leave his wig behind and we can all live in that!"

But a decision had to be made. Some mice suggested just moving a little way down the hill amongst the trees, but this sounded too dangerous and uncomfortable; the trees had been planted not long before, and there wasn't much undergrowth around them. Some liked the idea of abandoning the hill altogether and heading for the cookshops and chandlers' shops in Greenwich high street, but that would be a chancy business. There would be much dodging around people and cats, and probably most of the mice would be so scattered that they'd never come back to the hill at all.

Then someone pointed out that Flamsteed had said he was going to use the Queen's House, so if the mice moved there too they could keep an eye on him and would have a good chance of hearing about what was going on. True, it was a stone building so could be hard for mice to move around in, but it was rumoured to

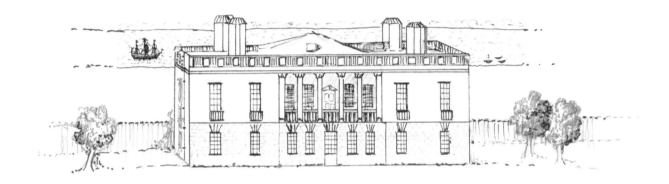

have good cellars. There was plenty of empty space upstairs, too, as there was no royal household there at present, though the mice had seen a few people coming and going from time to time.

So the following evening, once dusk had fallen, the mice scuttled down the hill to the Queen's House. Fortunately there turned out to be an ill-fitting basement door giving access to the cellars, which were full of clutter left behind by previous residents and by builders who had worked on refurbishment. It was full of good

places for mouse-nests. And an area that was still in use as a store had stairs, which linked up with a kitchen and a route to all of the ground floor. A caretaker was living there, with half a loaf of bread left on an open shelf, but there was no sign at all of any caretaking cat. There also seemed to be a pleasant, richly oily smell in the air, and the mice soon sniffed out its source: a ground-floor room was being used as a painters' studio. The painters kept bottles of linseed oil to mix their colours. It doesn't take a determined mouse long to gnaw a cork out of a bottle to sample the contents.

The mice decided life here could have its pleasures, and settled in. It was just as well, because the next day there was much noisy activity at the top of the hill – the workmen had come back and begun clearing the site. A few days later Hooke was seen heading back that way, with a rolled-up plan in his hand and an assistant with a wooden box, which they guessed to contain something like Moore's surveying instrument. Then Flamsteed appeared again too, walking up from the river to the Queen's House with a companion, both of them carrying boxes and bags. Behind them strode a tall waterman with a wooden trunk on his shoulder. The caretaker led them all to a room on the south side of the house, with a view of the park and the hilltop.

For the next few days the mice watched Flamsteed closely and were impressed to find that he was quite often awake and busy at night, almost like an outsize mouse. When they went out in the late evenings to browse around the Queen's House grounds, they saw him on the southern balcony, bringing out his boxes and unpacking strange devices. There were two square-cut wooden tubes several feet long (one longer than the other), which he propped up on a kind of trestle and pointed at the sky. Sometimes he got out a heavy metal object on a stand, which he moved around as though it was pointing at the sky too. He had a notebook and pencil with him and a lantern, so that when it was really dark he could see to scribble down notes.

Now and again he carried all these things down to the grounds of the house instead, perhaps because he wanted to point the tubes in different directions without the house getting in the way. But he wasn't up and about like this every night. If it was a night with a mixture of clouds and clear intervals, he might go indoors, lie down on a straw mattress in one corner of his room, take a nap for a couple of hours then get up again to check the sky. But if the weather was more thoroughly cloudy and wet he went away and wasn't seen again until the morning. The mice guessed he had found more comfortable lodgings somewhere nearby.

They didn't know quite what to make of Flamsteed's astronomical activities. A young mouse called Celestine (who will be important in the later part of this story) paid particularly close attention; she learned from one of

his chats with a visitor that the tubes were called telescopes and were used for looking at stars in the sky and special wandering stars called planets. Often he seemed to be pointing the tubes at the moon, and one imaginative mouse suggested that maybe this was done to see if it was really made of cheese. But the older ones dismissed the idea. They said there could be no point in that at all unless someone could go there to taste it and even the maddest humans couldn't attempt that. So they remained generally puzzled as to what the purpose could be.

They were also deeply disappointed by the astronomer's eating habits: he seemed to live mostly on bread and cheese or bread and cold meat, with the occasional hot pie from a Greenwich pie-shop. More encouragingly, he sometimes became so absorbed in reading, writing and calculating that he forgot about food altogether and left a plate lying around for a mouse to empty. And once his sister visited and brought him a jar of honey, so for a while after that some of the bread-crumbs he dropped made an especially enjoyable mouse snack.

In the first few weeks, visitors turned up quite often. There was the man they had seen helping with Flamsteed's luggage, and he called in again every few days bringing messages and packages from Sir Jonas Moore. His name was Nick. And sometimes a dashing young man in a very fine coat with silver buttons appeared.

He seemed very enthusiastic about astronomy, asked lots of questions, had long discussions with Flamsteed and often stayed on to share in using the telescopes. Flamsteed was heard to greet him as Mr Halley ("Mr Hawley", as the name was pronounced in those days).

A few of the mice, encouraged by Celestine, tried listening to their conversations and learned some mysterious astronomical words – such as meridian, zenith, aperture, focus, ascension and declination. For a day or two they found it entertaining to use them – in such phrases as "my stomach is just upon the meridian for dinner," and "through this aperture I can see a small crust of bread," and "it appears to be at the zenith point of that cupboard" – but the fashion passed quickly. They soon decided most of the talk was much too far above their heads and most of them gave up paying any attention to it.

As the autumn wore on, the man with silver buttons and other visitors were seen less often, the Queen's House became very chilly and the mice started spending a lot of their time asleep. But then they were disturbed by the appearance of some boys. There were a couple of them aged about fourteen, who started arriving together one day a week. Flamsteed told them they had to learn about trigonometry (whatever that was) and how to make calculations, and then to stay on through the evening and practise making

observations, when the sky was clear. They did this a few times, but the darker and colder it became the keener they were on finishing their tasks and leaving as fast as they could. Flamsteed just sighed and let them go.

In December another, smaller boy arrived; he was brought down to Greenwich by Sir Jonas and turned out to be Sir Jonas's grandson. He was called Jonas too, and can't have been more than about nine years old; but he seemed to be good at arithmetic and very interested in the telescopes.

Just before Christmas there was something special happening which meant sitting up late to watch the moon, and the mice heard Flamsteed talk to Jonas about it. He said that because the other boys wouldn't stay late on such a cold night he was relying on him to be his assistant. Jonas said he would and that he wasn't worried about getting cold. He sat up alone for a while, as the night started out cloudy and Flamsteed went off somewhere else to go to sleep.

Jonas didn't seem to be at all nervous about being on his own in the dark with only a lantern for company, but sat wrapped in a blanket by the window next to the balcony, looking out at the park and munching biscuits. (The mice heard some crumbs drop, and ate them in the morning.) From time to time he picked up the lantern and went outside, but soon came back again. It seemed to be a long while before he looked outside and didn't come back but went off to fetch Flamsteed.

Jonas was soon taken away again by his family, but in the following April a new assistant appeared. He looked a lot older than little Jonas, but not quite so old as Halley – maybe about fourteen or fifteen? – and his name was Tom Smith. He could write and do maths, in a way that earned him approving nods from Flamsteed; but he didn't seem to know much about astronomy. So Flamsteed was often busy teaching Tom and explaining the tasks where his help was needed.

CHAPTER 6

In which the Observatory is nearly finished
and a sketcher arrives to start drawing pictures

The new building was now beginning to look as though it must be nearly complete. The boundary fence had been replaced by a solid-looking brick wall. The building inside it now had a roof and some long windows, and a pair of turrets with little domes. A pair of owls arrived in the evenings to perch on the turrets. The mice called them Old Noll and Eliza, after the late Protector Cromwell and his wife, because of Old Noll's solemn expression and tendency to make them feel nervous.

Early on a sunny day towards the end of April, a few mice who were out in the Queen's House garden sniffing the fresh morning air saw a strange procession passing by. There were two horse-drawn carts, one supporting each end of a massive wooden pole that looked rather like a ship's mast. Beside the mast was a long square-cut wooden tube, rather like the ones Flamsteed used for his telescopes but a lot longer. The carts came in through one of the side gates of the park, and when they reached the foot of the hill the mast was rolled off the carts onto the ground, attached to chains and dragged up the grass steps behind the horses. The wooden tube was carried up on the shoulders of a line of workmen.

A day or two later, when Flamsteed was working on some calculations, there was a knock on the door and the housekeeper showed in a cheerful, military-looking man. He bowed briskly and said "Robert Thacker, sketcher of fortifications to the Ordnance Office, at your service."

Flamsteed left his desk, looking a little puzzled, bowed in his turn and said "I am at yours, but where are the fortifications?"

"I've come from Sir Jonas," explained the visitor, "who has asked me to make sketches of the Observatory so that Mr Place can engrave them."

"Ah yes," said Flamsteed, "he told me about that plan. But is this the time to begin on it, while the building isn't finished and there are no instruments in place?" "I believe so," came the reply. "I can start by drawing a view of the front from the foot of the hill and then take some other external views. I understand that the mast will be raised on the first of May, so I can easily add it in to the pictures that are finished by then. Sir Jonas is keen to have some of them ready by the end of the month, to show off to visitors at the eclipse. Then I can come back to see the interior and the instruments once they have arrived."

"He plans to turn the eclipse into a great event," said Flamsteed, with a sigh, "though I fear that the place won't be ready to move into properly until some weeks after that. I'm told that the King will attend, though probably at the last moment he'll remember a pressing engagement somewhere else and fail to turn up. But we may see a few courtiers, and certainly some members of the Royal Society.

"It's just as well that the decision was made to add summerhouses at either end of the front wall, although they weren't on the original plan. We can use one of those as a camera obscura, casting the sun's image through a hole in a shutter and through one of my smaller telescopes onto a screen. Perhaps you should draw that? The major instruments and clocks I believe will be installed in the course of the summer. But now I can at least show you where they will be placed, so you can decide what to include."

But then he added "Just give me a few moments to finish off this calculation," and sat down again with his papers. Now, the mice who were listening from their hidden corner included a few young ones who were adventurously inclined. They noticed that Flamsteed had left his coat lying on the bed quite

close to them. It hung down so that a pocket gaped at them temptingly, suggesting a way of gaining a free lift up to the top of the hill and a view of the new building. "Dare you!" said one, and two more, named Peggy and Percy, caught each other's eye and accepted the dare. Neither Flamsteed nor Thacker noticed them as they leapt into the pocket. Fortunately they found it was empty apart from containing a clean handkerchief and a penknife.

The other mice who had seen and heard all this scurried hastily back to the cellar to report the news. It didn't go down very well, mostly owing to puzzlement over what "the mast will be raised" might mean and what an eclipse might be to warrant such enthusiasm. It was evidently something to do with the sun, but opinion was divided as to whether the sun might stop moving, or turn a corner, or get bigger or smaller, or turn a different colour.

Some were worried that whatever happened it might be dangerous, and were sure that it would be safest not to explore until the human visitors had gone away. Indeed, they insisted that there would be no point at all in climbing all the way to the top of the hill for some while yet, as the building wasn't ready to move into. There was much tut-tutting from the elders about the rashness of the two who had gone off in the astronomer's pocket, though this was mixed with eager curiosity to hear what they would have to report if and when they got back again.

CHAPTER 7

In which two very bold mice get a close look at the new building

Peggy and Percy found themselves swung around rather alarmingly in Flamsteed's pocket as the astronomer and his visitor strode up the hill. But then things settled down and they were able to see glimpses of their surroundings through the opening of the pocket as well as sensing them in other ways.

First they saw a fraction of the outer brick wall of the Observatory site and the frame of the door Flamsteed opened. Then he crossed a paved yard, where his footsteps sounded quiet; then he went up a few solid steps to a door of the new building. Inside there were stairs which led to a large room, where voices echoed and footsteps sounded loudly on the wooden floorboards. There was a strong smell of fresh-cut wood and sawdust. Thacker sneezed.

Flamsteed said "This is the chief room. Portraits of the King and the Duke of York will be hung on that wall; the clocks will be housed nearby behind the

wainscot, where there's plenty of room for their thirteen-foot pendulums." "Do you mean there will be clock-faces thirteen feet up on the wall?" said Thacker. "How would you ever tell the time from those?" "No, no," replied Flamsteed, with a laugh. "These clocks will be of a very special new design, with the pendulums hung above the clock movements, so the clock faces can be at a height where everyone can see them easily."

As he turned around, the mice had a glimpse of honey-coloured wooden panelling and a section of a tall window with small panes of shiny new glass. "Will you keep other instruments in here?" asked Thacker. "Probably not," came the reply. "There is a small side room where I shall put my books and store most of the smaller instruments. But I can set a few things up here for you to draw them – a telescope mounted at one of the windows, perhaps, and my quadrant on its stand." "That would be ideal," said Thacker, "once the dust has been cleaned up and the portraits and clocks are in place."

"The larger instruments are to be housed outside," said Flamsteed. "The rest of the rooms here, below this one, are for me to live in, as the Astronomer Royal. Then there's a workshop at the back and a kitchen in the basement." The mice were keen to see those, but instead the two men went outside again, through the paved yard and into the grounds behind the building. There the earth had been churned up and piled with the builders' rubbish, so Flamsteed picked his way carefully across it.

"This is where the mast for the long telescope will stand," he explained, stepping over an obstacle (it was actually one end of the mast). A few paces further on he stopped, in a place where the mice could see nothing at all through the top of the pocket but a piece of hazy light blue sky. He said "this may not look at all important, but when it's completed it will be the most valuable part of the Observatory. The wall whose footings you see there is in the meridian, running exactly North-South, and the mural quadrant Hooke is designing will hang upon it. That will be ten feet across and, if it works as well as he claims, it will be a marvellous instrument, the most accurate in the world. The walls on either side will create two rooms, one to protect the quadrant and one for a large sextant. They'll be roofed with wood with sliding shutters, which can be opened to the sky." "I'll come back here to draw everything when it's all set up," said Thacker, "and maybe by then there'll be a little less mud."

"Let's go back into the park now," said Flamsteed, "and I'll show you the well we're using to house a long telescope." They left by the gate they had come in by, turned to the right and walked for some distance over the tussocky grass of the hilltop. Where they paused, some noises could be heard – muffled creaking, scraping and tapping sounds and a murmur of voices, which seemed to come from below the ground. The mice saw a frame of poles with a rope going round a pulley, as though something heavy was being let down on the rope. "It's about a hundred feet deep," said Flamsteed, "so once the builders have installed a spiral stairway it will be ideal for trying out one of the long-focus lenses that Sir Jonas has obtained from France. The middle of the spiral will act like a telescope tube."

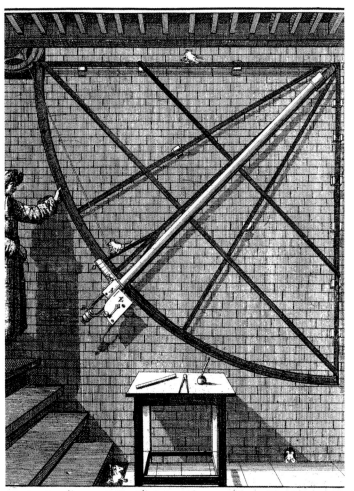

Quadrans Muralis Merid: 10 pedum Rad:

"Can it be dry enough for that?" asked Thacker. "It is lined with brick," came the reply, "and it will be utterly dark, which should mean that any star passing over the top of it can be observed in the daytime. Hooke tried something similar with a tube set up vertically at Gresham College, but it didn't work very well. The hope is that tiny variations in the star position will show a parallax effect, proving that the earth moves in an orbit and Copernicus was right."

"And for that you plan to climb a hundred feet down into the earth, in the dark, to make observations?" said Thacker, in horror. "Rather you than me! I hope you can show me a sketch of it on paper, so I can copy that and don't have to venture there myself."

After that they walked back down to the Queen's House together and Thacker left. Flamsteed threw his coat back onto the bed and went back to writing and calculating, and Peggy and Percy were able to slip out of the coat pocket unobserved. Then went to find the rest of the mice and tried to explain what they'd seen and heard. Their description of the great room was quite vivid and at least they could promise there was proper living accommodation on the floors below. More precise information could wait, as they'd heard Flamsteed declare that the most important part wasn't finished so it definitely wasn't time yet for any of them to move back.

CHAPTER 8

In which the mice see a mast raised and an eclipse happen; they appoint their own "Astronomouse"

From dawn onwards on 1st May the park was unusually busy and noisy, with large groups of young people frolicking about and singing, and waving branches at each other. A little later in the morning the mice saw several people they recognised making their way up the hill in a rather more sober fashion. Sir Jonas came by and with him the bewigged Sir Edward, and some kind of senior clergyman and several other well-dressed and self-important-looking men. A few minutes later Hooke and Sir Christopher appeared, leading a gang of workmen. Nick and the young man with silver buttons arrived together, called at the Queen's House and came out again with Flamsteed. They all made their way up the hill and disappeared into the Observatory. A southerly wind must have been blowing that day, as the murmur of voices carried down towards the Queen's House.

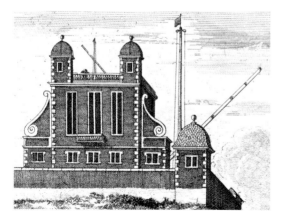

After a while a kind of heave-ho chanting started, and after a while more the top of the mast began to appear behind the Observatory building. It moved jerkily from a sloping to an upright position, and then a cheer went up. More chanting followed, and then one end of the wooden tube appeared, as if it had been hauled to about halfway up the pole and was slanting across it, though it wasn't all visible from the foot of the hill. Later they saw the people who had been there strolling back down the hill, all looking quite pleased with what had been accomplished.

After that, everything began to seem rather unsettled. Flamsteed never sat down to write for long, but often left to sprint up the hill and check on the builders' progress. For a few days before the eclipse, he was busy cleaning and adjusting his instruments and sorting out books and papers, which he packed in a box. On the day before, Nick and Halley turned up and helped to carry all these valuables up to the Observatory. They needed a second trip with a barrow to move Flamsteed's clock, which he seemed to be rather anxious about. On the day itself, Flamsteed disappeared up the hill at the crack of dawn, and the mice wandered outside and right to the edge of the Queen's House grounds on the side towards the Observatory, to watch for passers-by. They couldn't help hoping that the King would appear.

It was grey and cloudy to start with. Sir Jonas Moore came past very early on with half a dozen bigwigs; they seemed to be looking at the sky a lot and shaking their heads at the weather. After that it gradually began to look a little brighter, with some gaps between the clouds, and more and more people climbed the hill, mostly fashionably-dressed people arriving in twos and threes and even some families with their children. It was still not much beyond breakfast-time (just before eight o'clock, in fact) when the clouds finally melted away and the sun came out.

It didn't seem to be casting a very strong light and the young mouse called Celestine claimed that when it was still hazy with cloud (the one time when it was safe to look directly at the sun) it seemed to have a dark half-circle on one side. But since no-one else had been looking at that moment the idea was dismissed by the rest. They didn't see any of the other strange effects they had imagined. The park

was very quiet and peaceful for a while, in its slightly dim sunshine, and then the clouds came back. This time it became totally cloudy and stayed that way for more than an hour.

Soon the visitors started to reappear, strolling back down the hill, looking quite happy and talking to each other in a lively manner, as though they had just seen something worth talking about. A little later on the sun came out again quite brightly, and soon after that Flamsteed came back down the hill, with a few other people helping to carry his clock and instruments. He seemed quite happy too. But at the end of it all the mice were left feeling puzzled and disappointed because nothing seemed to have happened to the sun at all. They were especially sad that they hadn't seen anyone who looked majestic enough to be the King.

But, along with feeling puzzled and disappointed, the mice were now convinced that there was something really important going on. The new Observatory was clearly going to be a famous and much-visited place. And that mixture of thoughts led to one very important result. When the mice were together one day in a corner of the Queen's House painters' studio, just waking up from a comfortable nap under some canvasses, a few of them started grumbling about life and said perhaps they should all just stay with the painters and their pictures of ships, because moving back to the Observatory wouldn't be easy – there seemed to be only one door in the

outer wall, so how were they going to get in without being seen? Some of the younger mice replied that it would be fun to have a whole new building to live in, and easy enough to go wherever the humans did. Clarinda said firmly "our ancestors always lived on Greenwich Hill, with that wonderful view, and it would be such a shame to give it up." Then the grumblers said that if they moved back up the hill they were always going to be puzzled and confused by what was going on there, which would spoil everything.

And then Christopher was struck by an inspiration. "If we want to share in the Observatory's glory and fame and have everything explained to us so we can really enjoy it," he said, "we must appoint our own astronomer mouse." "The Astronomouse Royal!" someone else said, and laughed, and everyone could immediately see that this was a brilliant idea.

"Who should it be?" was the next question. It would need to be a mouse old enough to look dignified, but young enough not to doze off when there were any interesting visitors to see or observations going on. There was a lull in the conversation and some were just beginning to think that it might be easier to drop the subject and put off deciding after the next meal, when a small voice said "Would it help to have someone who can remember all Flamsteed's long words?"

It turned out that the owner of the voice, Celestine, could do that extraordinarily well, all the way from "aperture" to "zenith distance". She was fascinated by the instruments and had watched closely when Flamsteed was using them. She was also especially fond of his bookshelf, and had picked up a few good phrases like "the equation of time", "the doctrine of the sphere", or even "Ephemerides Bononienses Mediceorum", by browsing among the books and chewing their corners thoughtfully from time to time.

So a cheer went up, and the first Astronomouse Royal was unanimously elected.

CHAPTER 9

In which everyone moves back up the hill
to the new Royal Observatory

After that the days passed quickly. Flamsteed began to tell any callers that he'd soon be moving to the Observatory. He fidgeted about a good deal and rarely sat at his desk for long before going off to check what was happening at the top of the hill. He often went up there in the early mornings, taking Tom Smith with him; from their conversations the mice gathered this was something to do with looking at the sun and counting spots.

This sounded rather alarming - had the eclipse set off some sort of ailment that was bringing the sun out in measles? But Celestine, the Astronomouse, reassured them that Flamsteed wasn't at all worried about what was happening. It was just that there were a few dark spots and he wanted to know how long it would be before they went away again. So the mice relaxed and soon forgot about it.

And Flamsteed had plenty else to occupy his mind. After muttering a lot to himself or to the caretaker about mistakes made by the builders, he moved on to fretting about sloppy painters and unreliable delivery-men failing to bring pieces of furniture. He started packing up his trunk and boxes more than once, but generally had to half-unpack them again almost straight away, when there were things he needed.

Around the start of July some of the mice were quietly rummaging in a corner of the housekeeper's pantry when they overheard Flamsteed telling the housekeeper that tomorrow would be his day for moving out. So they had a sudden panic and realised they now really had to decide how they would manage to move out too.

The two mice who had travelled in Flamsteed's coat pocket were keen to do so again; the best idea the rest could come up with was to hide in some of his boxes and bundles. So very early next morning they explored the possibilities. The trunk they dismissed as too solid and hard to escape from – what if no-one opened the lid for days? But then the Astronomouse noticed that Flamsteed's brass quadrant had been detached from its stand and wrapped up in several layers of sacking, tied round with string. The telescopes had been turned into a long parcel in a similar sort of way. Where the sacking was bunched up it made folds and pockets of just the right size for mice.

So, before Flamsteed was awake, that's where most of them lodged themselves. The boldest two made a swift beeline for the pocket of the coat, which he'd left hanging on the back of a chair. A few more couldn't make up their minds until they saw the housekeeper bring in a wicker basket containing a loaf of bread and cold meat and crockery wrapped in brown paper. While Flamsteed was occupied with some piece of repacking, the last few mice scrambled over the edge of the basket and hid amongst the paper with the comforting smell of bread.

Soon afterwards Nick and Halley arrived, bringing with them a man whom Nick introduced as Cuthbert Denton. Cuthbert, he said, was being lent by the Ordnance Office as a labourer, to be an extra pair of hands to help Flamsteed at the Observatory. Cuthbert nodded and said nothing; he looked rather glum.

Flamsteed had collected extra books and instruments since he arrived at the Queen's House, so it took several trips for them to carry everything up the hill and into the new building. Fortunately they took the instrument bundles and the food basket first, and put everything down in a heap on the floor of the Octagon Room. So when they went back down the hill for the second batch of luggage, the mice had plenty of time to slip out of their hiding places and head downstairs. The two in Flamsteed's coat pocket found themselves with an uncomfortable double journey, as he kept his coat on until the end of the second trip; but after that he left it on a chair while he started moving boxes to different rooms. Then they were able to creep out of the pocket and down a chair-leg.

When they caught up with the other mice in the basement kitchen, they found them feeling a little discouraged. Taking a brief look at all the rooms had shown there was nothing there at all like the Queen's House cellars. There was a bedroom, containing a bed and a table with a jug and bowl on it to serve as a washstand; another room had a small dining table and a few wooden chairs and a buffet cupboard (like a sideboard, but taller).

A wide empty passageway gave on to a laundry-room with a copper (for heating water) and a sink, and another workroom with a trestle table and some shelves. The kitchen, on the floor below, had a table, a fireplace and bread-oven, shelves and a cupboard. In all this there didn't seem to be any place for mice at all – the brick and plaster walls were very solid, the skirting-boards were firmly tacked down and the cupboards were neatly made with no gaps round the doors.

So Christopher made a suggestion. "When we were down at the Queen's House," he said, "we mostly lived downstairs, but now we're going up in the world we should aim higher, closer to the stars. There must be a space under the roof."

For a moment being close to the stars sounded wonderfully romantic, and very suitable for the Astronomouse Royal. But then they thought about the height of the roof and how awkward it might be to reach the kitchen for a food supply, and even Celestine sighed and shook her head. Finally, Clarinda the history mouse came up with a solution, reminding them that they had once thought they could move back to their nests in the old foundations. Previous generations of mice had solved a similar problem when the building was rebuilt and altered, and that must have been how it was done. If they now had a look outside, they might find shelter near to the side door from the passage, and that would be convenient for the kitchen.

With this cheering thought they settled down to sleep in the bread-oven, thinking no-one would come that way for a good while. They waited until the very late evening, when Nick and Halley had finished helping Flamsteed move his boxes around and Flamsteed had done some unpacking and gone to bed.

Then, when it seemed absolutely quiet everywhere, the mice roused themselves and made for the side door. Here they found a narrow gap at the back edge, below the hinges of the door, so they set about gnawing and nibbling at the wood to turn it into a slightly bigger gap. Soon there was space to get through.

Outside they found the air was cool and fresh, much pleasanter than the indoor sawdust-and-paint smells. They sniffed it a few times, checked that there was no sign of the owls being about, and set off to tour the outside of the building. The brickwork at the foot of the walls turned out to be tidy, with only a few small nooks and crannies here and there, and a single dusty fragment of an old mouse-nest.

But on the west side of the building, near some ground that had been dug over for a kitchen garden, they found something much more interesting. There was a lead water-tank set close to the house wall, with a pump for drawing water. It was set upon some rows of bricks with spaces in between and there was a narrow, tall space between it and the wall.

Christopher, their nest-building expert, suddenly seemed to wake up (until then he'd still been secretly daydreaming about the roof). All the mice could immediately see that the spaces under the tank would provide good shelter. They had a little difficulty with lining materials, but eventually found some ragged pieces of cloth dropped by the workmen who'd been cleaning the windows. These they tore and chewed up a bit, and made into a comfortable lining for nests.

CHAPTER 10

In which the mice begin to feel at home, and the Observatory's instruments arrive

Over the next few days and weeks the mice found this arrangement worked very well. They could easily slip into the house by the edge of the side door whenever they wanted, and just as easily slip out again. From there they worked their way around the building, creating routes behind the cupboards and the skirting-boards, and behind the panelling in the Great Room. Outside they explored the summer-houses and the separate small building in the garden, which was still being finished.

They were reminded about what that was for when Flamsteed went out there to nag the workmen and told them it had to be ready for two large instruments to arrive, a quadrant and a sextant. These had cost Sir Jonas a great deal of money and were very delicate and fragile and the only ones of their kind in the world, so they were going to be provided with somewhere dry and safe to live. The Astronomouse was thrilled at this idea, but she had some difficulty in convincing the others.

When the clocks and large instruments began to arrive there was a lot of fuss and to-ing and fro-ing by all sorts of people. Sir Jonas and his friends came by, instrument-makers and the instrument-makers' errand-boys, and workmen carrying parcels and boxes, as well as Flamsteed and Tom and Cuthbert, and sometimes Halley too.

At the busiest times the mice chose their hiding-places carefully and stayed away from the noise, but when Flamsteed was working quietly on adjusting instruments or explaining them to his assistants, they sent the Astronomouse to creep closer and find out what was happening.

The powerful brassy, oily smell that hung around the large instruments at first seemed rather horrible, but the mice soon started to get used to it.

Very early one morning, when they were absolutely sure there was no-one around to see them, they all went down to the sextant house for a closer look. As they found some steps in place, they managed to climb up to the curved edge of the sextant and slide down it, and a few of the bolder mice enjoyed going mountaineering amongst its supporting spokes and framework.

The great quadrant proved a little harder to tackle (see p. 31).

Because the clocks were installed behind the wooden panelling, all the mice found them both worrying and rather fascinating. Flamsteed seemed to think the same, and was often in the octagon room watching the dials, comparing them with each other and jotting down notes. The mice had just begun to get used to the way the clockwork noise carried all through the woodwork, when it began to change: some creaking was heard, and first one clock stopped, and then the other.

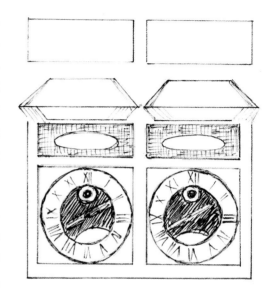

Flamsteed became quite agitated and summoned the clockmaker, young Mr Thomas Tompion, who solemnly came in and opened the panelling with a key, cleaned and adjusted something inside and got the clocks going again. This happened several times, with Flamsteed getting crosser each time and repeatedly asking the clockmaker why he couldn't have a key himself.

In the end the Astronomouse overheard him complaining about it to Sir Jonas and Sir Jonas must have persuaded Mr Tompion. So after that, Flamsteed had his own key and started looking less worried. The clocks stopped less often and he generally got them going again quite quickly. For a little while the mice kept up the habit of pausing to have a look at the clocks when they were passing that way, but eventually they began taking them for granted.

While all this was going on, Robert Thacker the sketcher appeared again and began drawing, starting with a view of the Octagon Room with the clocks. He sat still in one place, resting a piece of paper on a board balanced on his knee, and told the other people he summoned to stay still too. That meant that the Astronomouse and a few other mice felt quite comfortable watching them from under one of the chairs that stood against the wall.

46

Thacker told Flamsteed to stand next to his quadrant, and then nothing seemed to happen for a long time except the occasional murmur of conversation; the mice went to sleep.

They opened an eye to see Flamsteed being sent away and someone else being asked to sit at a small table by the back wall and pretend to be writing. Then there was another long pause before he was allowed to move and another person was brought in to sit at a telescope, which was set up with one end poking through the window and the other on a kind of bench-shaped stand. It took some fussing about by Flamsteed and the others to get it there. The mice kept very quiet and still while this happened, as it was all rather close to where they were hiding; they couldn't see much, but could tell what was going on from people's voices. They guessed it was Tom Smith doing the writing and Halley sitting at the telescope. It seemed a long while before the sketcher was satisfied and let the young men leave their places.

Then for a few more days the mice kept coming across Thacker and his sketchbook around the Observatory, as he wandered about between the quadrant house and sextant house, the summer-houses at the ends of the walls,

and various corners of the grounds, drawing busily. Then he disappeared again and life settled down, although the regular routine of observing at night and writing up results in the daytime was still sometimes interrupted, either by bad weather or by the arrival of visitors. The mice noticed that Flamsteed didn't seem to mind callers too much if they arrived during a spell of bad weather, and in any case he was always polite to them and showed them around. But if it was fine weather and he'd been observing the night before they sometimes heard him complaining crossly to Tom about being woken up, or about being disturbed by "gawpers" when he was working.

The Astronomouse kept up her habit of dozing during the daytime behind a row of books on a shelf in Flamsteed's study, where there was a pleasant warm smell of leather bindings. Through this she happened to overhear Flamsteed muttering to himself as he wrote letters to Sir Jonas, especially when he was worried and trying to find tactful phrases to report bad news. It appeared that the longest telescope – the one on the mast – was being abandoned because it was too shaky, the telescope in the well was no use because it was too damp, and the great brass quadrant didn't work very well either. Its arm had jerked in some way and nearly cut off Cuthbert's fingers. But there must still be some instruments that worked: Flamsteed and Tom and Cuthbert spent a lot of evenings and nights in the sextant house, or sat up on the Observatory roof with the telescopes and other instruments that had been brought from the Queen's House.

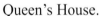

For a little while the mice benefited from the failure of the longest telescope. Its boxy wooden tube was left lying along one side of the yard for quite a long time, so as soon as the Astronomouse told them it was no longer wanted, they started living in it. It was rather warmer in the winter than their previous place under the water-tank, and they made a warm and comfortable nest-lining from chewed-up pieces of one of the ropes that had been attached to the mast.

CHAPTER 11

In which pictures of the Observatory appear and are very much admired – despite their containing no mice

One morning late in the autumn, Sir Jonas and Nick arrived. When Tom opened the door to them, Sir Jonas strode in looking rather pleased with himself and said to Flamsteed "The engravings are finished!" Nick followed carrying a large flat package under one arm. Flamsteed quickly led them to his study, where Nick put the package down on a table and Sir Jonas opened its paper wrapping with a flourish and started taking the contents out. The noise of the people arriving woke up Celestine and several other mice who had been dozing at the back of the bookshelf; they peered out from a couple of spaces between the books and got a good view.

"Place has done a fine job," said Sir Jonas. "Here's an elegant title page, a map of the park showing how the Royal Observatory is situated, and a plan of the building and grounds. Then there's a view of the front of the Observatory, taken from the foot of the hill, and more views from every side, with the river and the city in the background. Inside, here's the Octagon Room, with the clocks, and the quadrant house and sextant house – two views of the sextant – and one of the summer-houses set up for observing the sun. The picture of the well telescope has extra drawings added to fill the space, as it's so long and thin, so there was a chance to include a few smaller devices in the space beside it. It all seems to me very clear and well done. I'll leave this copy with you so you can show it to visitors."

Flamsteed nodded appreciatively at the appearance of each sheet, and smiled when he saw himself in the Octagon Room picture. At the end he said "Very fine indeed, Sir Jonas. A worthy record of your great generosity, and of course of His Majesty's."

Then they all left together, leaving the pictures on the desk. After a moment or two, when the sound of voices had faded away, the mice jumped down from the bookshelf to take a closer look. They were thrilled to know that they were living somewhere that had been put into fine pictures with so much black printing-ink, and that so many people would be made to admire the results. The views of the great room and the sextant house happened to be the easiest to see at the top of the spread-out pile, so they had a good look at those and enjoyed recognising everything they saw.

They had seen a few painted pictures before, of course – the portraits of the King and his brother that now hung in the Observatory, and the pictures of ships that were painted in the Queen's House – but to see realistic pictures of somewhere they knew so well was an amazing experience. For a brief moment they thought they should see themselves in all the pictures too and were disappointed not to, but then they remembered why it just wasn't possible. One or two still imagined that they *could* have been drawn too if they had crept into Thacker's line of view very quietly, and said that if he came again he should at the very least be persuaded to draw in the Astronomouse.

Seeing the new pictures suddenly made them remember that this place they had got used to living in was really a Royal Observatory and perhaps even more special than they had realised. The people there must be very special too, because they appeared in the pictures. For the next few days they found it hard to settle calmly to anything, but all took to following Flamsteed around and watching him closely with something like awe. He seemed rather more cheerful than he had been for a while, and at least once a day he looked through the pictures again or showed them to Tom.

Because the mice were keeping such a close eye on Flamsteed, they were all there on the roof, somewhere around the foot of the balustrade, in the early evening a couple of days after the pictures had arrived. It had been a fine day and was not yet quite dusk, and Flamsteed and Tom had come up there to check that there were no clouds on the horizon. A little later on they set up a telescope. But first they stood and leaned on the rail and gazed out westwards, where there were no clouds at all, but fine views of Greenwich town and the river and the city of London.

"It's a great city, Tom," said Flamsteed, "rising again after the Great Fire, with a noble king and many curious and ingenious citizens. And now, thanks to the pictures so well drawn by Mr Thacker and engraved by Mr Place, all the world can see that the King has his Royal Observatory, just like the French. I do believe it will be truly worthy of that name. We can't rival Paris in the size of the building, of course, but we have a finer site and a splendid sextant and the best clocks in the world, thanks to Sir Jonas. As the King's astronomer, I can make observations in a regular way, and in a few years there will be more of them than any Englishman has ever made before. Somehow − by the moon moving against the stars, or by the planets, or the satellites of Jupiter − I am sure we can arrive at a method of finding longitude at sea, as His Majesty commands. And that will bring us glory indeed."

Tom nodded happily; he seemed rather at a loss for words, but eventually said
"I hope all that will happen while I am here helping with the work."

The mice could understand how impressed Tom must be with Flamsteed's talk of glory and being the best in the world, because they felt quite carried away by it too. They quickly went down to one of their favourite hiding-places, in the space between the ceiling of the great room and the roof (the place where Christopher had once suggested they should live). When they were all there, they jostled about a little and all looked at the Astronomouse in a hopeful kind of way, so she could tell that she was expected to make a speech. And this is what she said:

"Mice of Greenwich Hill, of Greenwich Castle and now of the Royal Observatory, you have just heard what Mr Flamsteed, the King's astronomer has said about how wonderful this place is and what important work it is going to do. We shall be here to see that happen – playing our part by keeping Flamsteed and his assistants company and admiring their achievements. We can listen respectfully to their conversations with distinguished visitors and provide a proper reception for any foreign mice who may travel in the visitors' baggage. Then tales about the Observatory will be spread throughout the world. So it is a very good thing that we were bold enough to come back to this extraordinary place. It would not be the same without us." Much applause followed.

The Astronomouse Royal was, of course, to be the first in a long and continuing line of mice with a special knowledge of and attachment to astronomy. The Astronomers Royal have since stopped running the Observatory and have left Greenwich altogether, but the mice are still there.

HISTORICAL NOTES

This story is based on real events –
the founding and building of the Royal Observatory
at Greenwich in 1675-76 – but all the conversations are made up

The Real People in this History

In order of appearance (or of being mentioned):

- Sir Christopher Wren (1632-1723), architect and Surveyor of the King's Works. Earlier in life he was a professor of astronomy, first at Gresham College in London and then in Oxford. After the Great Fire of London he became famous as the designer of the new St Paul's Cathedral and many London churches

- Sir Jonas Moore (1618-79), Surveyor of the Royal Ordnance and Flamsteed's patron

- John Flamsteed (1646-1719), appointed Astronomer Royal in 1675

- Robert Hooke (1635-1703), Curator of Experiments to the Royal Society, instrument-designer, surveyor and architect. Wrote a diary, in which he briefly noted some of his trips to Greenwich and involvement with building the Observatory

- Thomas Tompion (1639-1713), clockmaker (later a very famous one)

- Sir Edward Sherburne (1618-1702), Clerk of the Royal Ordnance, a translator and writer on astronomy and a friend of Sir Jonas

- Nicholas Stephenson ('Nick') (?-1678), Second Clerk to Sir Jonas as Surveyor of the Ordnance

- Edmond Halley (1656-1742), a student at Oxford with a passion for astronomy. Much later (in 1720) he was to succeed Flamsteed as Astronomer Royal

- Jonas Hanway (about 1669-1737), Sir Jonas Moore's grandson (the son of his daughter Mary and her husband William Hanway)

- Thomas Smith (about 1662-about 1700), Flamsteed's first assistant at the Observatory

- Robert Thacker (around in 1674-80), at that time a sketcher in the Ordnance Office

- Francis Place (1647-1728), an artist and engraver

- Cuthbert Denton (around in 1676-80), an Ordnance Office labourer sent down from the Tower of London to assist Flamsteed

- And the King who never visited at all was Charles II (1630-1685); he reigned from 1649 or 1660 (depending on whether you count the years of Oliver Cromwell's rule), to 1685

Note on the title "Astronomus Regia"

This echoes one of the titles Flamsteed sometimes used as the King's astronomer – "Astronomicus Regius". But it has been adapted by employing the Latin word for a mouse, which is "mus".

This is unusual in that it can be taken as a masculine or feminine word without changing its form. A female word-ending has been used in the adjective "Regia" to reflect the gender of the first Astronomouse.

Any male successor would have been termed "Astronomus Regius".

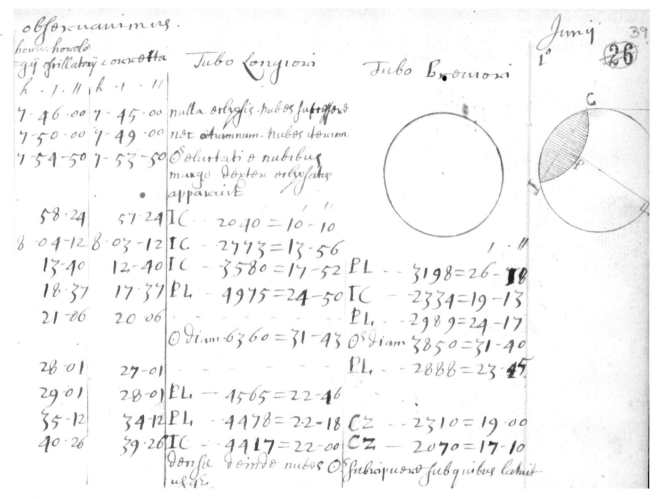

Flamsteed's neat copy of his notes on the solar eclipse of 1 June 1676 (RGO 1/13, f. 39r),
reproduced by kind permission of the Syndics of Cambridge University Library